# Maeve and Rob

### and

## ROB

### SHARING LOVERS EROTICA

# JUST PLAIN BOB

# WARNING

This book contains sexually explicit scenes and adult language. It may be considered offensive to some readers. This book is for sale to adults ONLY.

Please store your files wisely where they cannot be accessed by underage readers.

\* \* \* \* \* \* \* \* \* \* \* \* \* \* \* \* \* \* \*

## WANT FREE COPIES OF MY BOOKS?

Just visit my blog and download free copies of my books:

**awesomeauthors.org/justplainbob**

### About the Publisher

**4Fun Publishing,** a member of **BLVNP Incorporated**, 340 S. Lemon #6200, Walnut CA 91789, info@blvnp.com / legal@blvnp.com

NOTE: Due to the highly emotional reaction of some people to works of erotic fiction, any email sent to the above address that contains foul language or religious references is automatically deleted by our anti-spam software and will not be seen. All other communications are welcome.

### DISCLAIMER

Please don't be stupid and kill yourself. This book is a work of FICTION. Do not try any new sexual practice that you find in this book. It is fiction and not to be confused with reality. Neither the author nor the publisher or its associates assume any responsibility for any loss, injury, death or legal consequences resulting from acting on the contents in this book. Every character in this book is over 18 years of age. The author's opinions are not to be construed as the opinions of the publisher. The material in this book is for entertainment purposes ONLY. Enjoy.

# Maeve and Rob

## Sharing Lovers Erotica

By: Just Plain Bob

ISBN: 978-1-68030-516-6

# Chapter 1

It is my fault and I accept it. I don't try to blame anyone else. I allowed it to happen and up to the point where it went bad I was an active participant. If I blame it on anything, it would have to be love.

I fell head over heels in love with Maeve the first time I laid eyes on her. It was at a cocktail party that my company was throwing for our customers and suppliers. I was talking with the sales rep for the company that sold us some of the chemicals we use in our manufacturing process when she walked into the room. She was on the arm of a man I took an instant dislike to. Had never met, had never spoken to him, had never even heard of him, but my dislike was intense because she was with him and not me.

She was a fairly tall woman, maybe five foot seven or eight. Dirty blond hair that hung down below her shoulders. Very nice looking body, but I have to admit that I didn't spend much time trying to figure out her weight or measurements. It was her face that grabbed my attention. I don't know how to describe it. Her face had planes and angles. She looked an awful lot like porn star Krystal Summers. I couldn't take my eyes off of her. Suddenly there was a hand in front of my face, fingers snapping and a voice saying:

"Earth to Rob, Earth to Rob, come in please."

Charlie, the sales rep I had been talking to, chuckled and said:

"Obviously nothing that I have to say is going to register on you as long as she is in the room so I'll let you go. Call me in the morning."

Then he laughed and said, "Good luck" and walked toward the bar leaving me standing there staring at Maeve.

I was still staring at her when she turned her head and our eyes met. I felt a jolt all the way to the soles of my feet. She didn't smile at me or nod an acknowledgement; she held my eyes for a couple of seconds and then looked away. I spent the rest of the cocktail party watching her and making note of who she talked with so I could approach them later and in talking with them hopefully find out more about her.

I was standing at the bar waiting for the barmaid to build me a vodka tonic with lime when she walked up to stand next to me. She ordered a Cosmo and then turned to me and said:

"Do I have a big, nasty looking spot on my skirt or something like that?"

"Not that I noticed. Why?"

"Because every time I look your way you are looking at me."

Not being one to pass up an opening I said, "And at your age this comes as a surprise? You know you are drop dead gorgeous and that men, me among them, are going to be fascinated with you. I've spent most of the evening since you walked in trying to think of a way to meet you."

"Coming up to me and saying hello would work."

"I know, but it would be socially awkward since you are here with another guy."

"Why would it be awkward? You wouldn't say "Hello, I'd like to take you to bed," would you?"

"Of course not, but your date would know that my real purpose in coming up to you would be to try and separate you from him and that is what would make the situation awkward."

"Well fortunately for you he is just a date and he is replaceable and I just happen to have a soft spot for guys who find me fascinating."

She stuck out her hand and said, "Maeve Billings and I'll give you advance warning that I hate being called Mae."

I took her hand and carried it to my lips and lightly kissed it and said, "Rob. Rob Daltry."

"Nice meeting you, Rob. Although my date is replaceable he is still my date this evening and I need to get back to him." She started to walk away and then turned back to me.

"I'm in the book, Rob Daltry."

She turned and walked back to her date.

The next evening I called her and asked her to have dinner with me on Friday and she said she would love to.

Maeve owned me from the start. Our first date was all it took to tell me that I had found the woman I wanted to spend the rest of my life with. The first date led to a second and the second to a third. I longed to take her in my arms and make mad, passionate love to her, but I kept my hands to myself and behaved. I would do nothing that might scare her off or make her push me away.

At the end of our third date I walked Maeve to the door of her condo, told her that I'd had a lovely time and leaned forward to kiss her on the cheek and she put a hand on my chest to stop me.

"Do I have bad breath, Rob?"

"No, of course not."

"Then kiss me," and she put her arms around my neck and drew me to her. It was a long, passionate kiss and when we broke it she turned, unlocked and opened her door. Then she turned to me, took hold of my tie and pulled me along behind her. Once inside she turned and gave me another very passionate kiss and then said:

"I'm not the least bit old fashioned, Rob. I'm a very modern girl who goes after what she wants and right now what I want is you. The bedroom is back this way," and she turned and started walking away from me. She went eight or ten steps and then turned to look back at me standing there stunned at the suddenness of it all. "Coming?" she asked and then headed for her bedroom.

I finally got my act together and went after her. She was waiting for me when I came into the room and she smiled and said, "Good boy," and then she started to undress. There was no music and she didn't go through any of the movements that strippers use, but watching Maeve undress was one of the most erotic things that I had ever seen. First she shimmied out of her dress and let it fall and puddle around her feet. She smiled and looked into my eyes as she casually kicked the dress off to a corner and her hands went to her bra. The bra came off and she tossed it aside and still looking into my eyes she took off her panties and without looking tossed them over her shoulder. She stood in front of me in garter belt, nylons and high heels and said:

"Well?"

I looked at her confused and she said, "I seem to be the only one here undressed."

Things might have been going a little fast for me, but I wasn't stupid so I hurriedly undressed. As I stood there looking at her with eyes and heart full of desire I confessed;

"I'm scared. I'm scared that I might not do you justice. It has been a while for me and I could be kind of quick."

"Do your best, sweetie; we have all night."

I was quick, but it didn't seem to bother Maeve and she took my cock in her mouth and got me back up and then she took charge. She knew what she wanted and she led me along. Before the night was over I had eaten her pussy, savored her in the doggie position, received another superb blow job, had taken her anally and then we had showered together and then enjoyed sex in the missionary position. I fell asleep with my arms around her.

***

That started an on again/off again relationship that ran for almost two years. It was on again-off again because even though Maeve kept telling me that I was the man she wanted to settle down with she wasn't ready to settle down. I wasn't all that happy about it, but Maeve was a very forceful person and there was a lot of 'my way or the highway' in her and I was in no hurry to 'hit the road' as far as she was concerned so I took what I could get.

The first time she did it to me we had been dating for about six months. Actually dating wasn't the word for it. We basically lived together. After our first night of passionate sex we became an instant couple and she either slept at my apartment or I slept at her condo. Anyway, one evening I called her at work and asked her the usual question:

"What would you like to do for dinner and is tonight your place or mine?"

"Neither, honey. I have a date tonight."

"A date?"

"Yes."

"What kind of a date?"

"Dinner and then maybe dancing."

I was silent for a moment or two while I contemplated that and then I said, "Oh. Have a good time," and I hung up on her. The phone rang almost instantly and caller ID said that it was Maeve so I ignored it. I grabbed my keys and headed for The Extra Point which was a sports bar where my cousin George tended bar. I sat down at the bar and ordered a Black Jack with water back and then sat there being pissed. I thought that Maeve and I had something going, but I was obviously wrong about that. I had a couple of drinks at the bar and then some guys I knew came in and we shot pool until closing time.

The next day at work I debated calling Maeve at the advertising agency where she worked, but finally decided against it. She chose to break the bond between us and I had no real claim on her. Why call and make it look like I was begging.

A week went by and I got a call from Maeve. "Can I come over tonight?"

"No, I have a date tonight."

"A date?"

"Yeah. Dinner and maybe dancing."

"Maybe dancing?"

"Yeah, just maybe. She might want to do something else."

"Who is it? Do I know her?"

"I don't know. You might know her."

"What's her name?"

"Haven't got a clue, Maeve. I haven't met her yet, but I'm sure that I'll find her at one of the places I'll hit tonight. Got to go, Maeve. Bye."

I'd no sooner disconnected than the phone rang. Caller ID showed that it was Maeve and I wondered how she did that. It was the second time she had been able to get back to me instantly when I disconnected. It always seemed to take me twenty or thirty seconds to get back to someone who I was disconnected from. Oh well, one of life's little mysteries.

I grabbed my keys and headed for the Extra Point. I drank some, talked to George and shot some pool for a while. I headed home about eleven. When I walked into my apartment I turned on the light I found Maeve sitting on my couch.

"You're home kind of early. Date didn't go well?"

I shrugged, "Sometimes you get lucky and sometimes you don't. What's up with you? Tired of your new boyfriend already?"

"I don't have a new boyfriend. He was just a guy I met that I thought I wanted to get to know better."

"So why are you here?"

"Once I got to know him better I found that he wasn't worth the bother."

"That doesn't answer the question. Why are you here?"

"Because you are my guy. You going to make me leave?"

Looking back I guess that I should have made her leave, but I was hopelessly in love with her and so I said, "Of course not" and she stood up and said, "Take me to bed, baby. We have five days to make up for."

When Maeve finished with me I was so wiped out that I had to call in sick to work the next day. Her "date" was never mentioned again.

\*\*\*

Five months later it happened again only that time we had a date to go to a concert. I received a call from Maeve at work telling me that something had come up at work and she was going to have to cancel. She said she might be working late so she would just go on home to her condo that night. I didn't feel like going to the concert alone so I decided to get a bite to eat and then catch a movie.

I had eaten and I was driving down Madison on my way to the movie when I saw Maeve and a man I didn't recognize walking hand in hand into the Fleetwood Hotel. At first I thought she was having dinner with a client since she did tell me that something had come up at work, but then I remembered that the Fleetwood did not have a restaurant or a lounge – just rooms. And why would she be holding hands with a client?

I can't even remember the name of the movie I sat through and I don't remember all that much about the movie itself other than it had Reese Witherspoon in it. What I remember most about my time in that movie theatre was a constant replay of Maeve and the man walking into the Fleetwood together.

It was six days before I heard from Maeve again. She called me at work to ask if that night was going to be at her place or mine.

"How about neither. We can take a room at the Fleetwood. Got to go. Got another call on the other line."

That evening when I got off work I didn't go home. I went to the Extra Point and drank some, talked to George, but passed on shooting pool. When I got to my apartment I saw Maeve's Cherokee in the lot and I braced myself for the confrontation that was going to take place when I walked into my apartment. I loved Maeve, but I wasn't a doormat and I was not going to continue to let her wipe her feet on me. The first time I had let it go, but I wasn't going to do it again.

When I entered the apartment and hit the light switch I looked toward the couch expecting to see Maeve sitting there, but the couch was empty. Maeve was in the bedroom, naked and lying on top of the sheets waiting for me. Before I could say a word she said:

"Hurry baby, I need you; I need you right now."

When I hesitated she came off the bed, knelt in front of me, got my cock out and started sucking on it. "Confrontation can wait until after" I thought as I started to take off my shirt. The confrontation didn't come "after" because "after" I was so exhausted that I fell instantly asleep.

I woke up to the smell of frying bacon. I hopped into the shower and then got dressed for work. As I entered the kitchen Maeve was just setting the food on the table. The coffee was already poured and as I sat down Maeve said:

"Dig in. Eat hearty and have a good lunch. You will need all your strength tonight."

"Why are you trying to fuck me to death, Maeve? Didn't you get enough at the Fleetwood last week?"

"I never get enough, lover, but to answer your unasked question he meant nothing to me. You know I'm yours, baby, but I'm young, healthy and full of curiosity and the time to satisfy that curiosity is before marriage, not after."

"I know I'm a little late in asking, but do you use condoms when you are satisfying your curiosity?"

"That's a mean question to ask."

"No it isn't, Maeve. And the reason it isn't is because I have no curiosity. I'm not the least bit curious about what a venereal disease feels like so if you are not using protection while you are out there being curious I would prefer that you don't come to my bed after satisfying your curiosity until you have at least had yourself checked to make sure that you are disease free."

I finished my coffee and then got up and left. I didn't get the "your place or mine" call at work that day so I hit the Point on the way home from work for a few drinks and a few words with George. George was getting a tad tired of hearing me 'whine' about Maeve so he said;

"Walk away, Rob. Trust me on this, Cuz, it isn't worth it."

Easy for him to say since he wasn't head over heels in love with her. Maeve's car wasn't in the parking lot when I got there. I made myself some dinner, watched a thing about dinosaurs on the History channel and then went to bed early. I didn't hear her come in. The first I knew she was there was when her hot mouth woke up both me and my cock. It turned into another exhausting night and just before I fell asleep Maeve whispered:

"I'm sorry, baby; I promise that it won't happen again."

But two months later it did happen again and when I reminded her that she had promised me that it wouldn't happen again she told me that she had kept her promise and had made him use condoms. Then she told me to take her to bed and show her again why I was and would always be her main man.

"I don't want to be your main man, Maeve; I want to be your only man."

"You will be, baby, but not just yet. I'm not ready to settle down."

"But I am, Maeve, I am."

***

The next day I went apartment hunting, found one that I liked and three days later I took a day off work and moved. I did not tell Maeve. That evening my cell went off and the display showed that the call was from Maeve. I didn't answer it and let it go to voicemail. I waited a minute and then I listened to the voicemail.

"Rob, baby, I'm at your apartment and there is nothing here. What's going on?"

I shrugged and deleted the message. The next day I called my secretary into my office and told her not to put through any calls from Maeve. If Maeve called I was always to be out of the office or in an important meeting.

"I know it isn't fair to put you in the middle of my personal problems, but I'll make it worth your while. Lunch on me for you and three of your friends at the Hilton every Friday for a month. Deal?"

Donna smiled at me, stuck out her hand and said "Deal" and we shook on it.

I thought about Maeve every night as I drove home from work and wondered where she was. I thought about her as I fixed my dinner and watched TV and wondered where she was. At night I lay in bed looking up at the ceiling and thought of her and wondered where she was. When I woke up in the morning the first thing I saw was the empty side of the bed and I thought about her and wondered where she was. I loved the stupid cunt and I knew that getting over her was not going to be easy – if it could even be done – but I had no idea that it was going to be anywhere near as hard as it was.

Every day Donna would hand me a stack of message slips from Maeve and I would pitch them into the trash. My cell collected ten or twelve missed messages and voice mails every day and I deleted them. George called me and told me Maeve had been in asking about me and she was asking everyone who knew me if they knew where I was. No one did because I'd told no one. I didn't frequent the bars and restaurants that I used to go to and I even went so far as to bribe the security guys in the lobby of the building to alert me any time Maeve came around. That paid off and several times I had to leave the building in the evenings through the loading dock. Several times I got phone calls telling me that Maeve was sitting in the parking lot waiting for me to get to work in the morning.

*** 

I managed to avoid all contact with Maeve – for all of two months. And then one evening I came home from work to my new apartment and found Maeve waiting for me. Before she could say a word I asked:

"How did you find me?"

"The old fashioned way. I hired a private detective."

"You can't be serious?"

"Oh but I am."

"You spent good money on a P.I? What in God's name for?"

"Because you ran and it was important to me to know where my main man was."

"I have no interest in being your main man. I told you that. Only man status is all I'm willing to go with."

"Can we go inside and talk about this? I mean it really isn't any business of your neighbors."

What the hell; she already knew where I lived so I opened the door and let her in.

"Why are you not able to understand that you are my man?"

"It is because I am not your man, Maeve. I don't know why you keep telling yourself that I am, but I obviously am not. If I was your man you wouldn't be fucking around with other men. What I am is someone you can use as a home base; someone you can fall back on when other things don't work out. Well I'm not going to be your fall back position any more. I once asked you to marry me and I accepted it when you said you weren't ready to settle down. I now realize that you will never be ready to settle down. You are always going to find some other guy you want to fuck for a while. Okay. I accept that is the way it is going to be, but I won't live like that. Now it is time for me to move on."

"You can't mean that, Rob, not after all we have meant to each other."

"I mean it, Maeve. It is time – hell, it is past time – for me to move on."

"Oh God, Rob; don't you realize that what we have now is almost perfect?"

"Maybe for you, Maeve, but not for me."

"Don't you realize that marriage would change everything?"

"In what way, Maeve? What would change other than I would go from being your man three quarters of the time to being your man full time? What would change other than your having to give up being curious and satisfying that curiosity?"

She was silent for several seconds and then she said, "You couldn't live with me full time, Rob; I'm too much of a controlling bitch. What was it you once told me? That I had a touch of "My way or the highway" in me? It is more than a touch, Rob, way more than a touch. I have to be in charge, Rob. My father was the original male chauvinistic pig. As far as he was concerned women were put on this Earth for one reason and one reason only – to serve men. Lick my boots, fetch my pipe and slippers, get into the kitchen and get dinner ready. Why my mother never killed him I'll never understand, but I grew up promising myself that I'd never let a man control me that way. Unfortunately I went too far the other way and became the female counterpart to my father. Although maybe not quite as bad.

"But I have a need to boss men around. The men I've gone out with since meeting you? In each of them I sensed a touch of the submissive so I dated them, pushed them around until I got sick of them and then walked away from them. As far as you being my base? That is partially true, but only partially. What you are, Rob, is my rock, my anchor. I need you, Rob. I love you and I have to be with you. I feel empty when you aren't there for me. These last two months I've been absolutely miserable. I need you, Rob; I really do need you."

"Your need changes nothing, Maeve. I meant what I said. I am not willing to be your 'main man'. It is 'only man' or nothing."

"We wouldn't last that way, Rob. I would try to boss you around and sooner or later you would get tired of it and sooner or later you would walk away from me."

"That is where we are now, Maeve. I am tired of your walking away from me and fucking other men and then coming back to me and acting as if it means nothing. Well maybe it means nothing to you, but I don't feel the same way and that is why I walked away from you two months ago."

I looked at her sitting there looking dispirited and I wanted to take her in my arms and comfort her, but I knew if I did I would be lost. On the other hand I loved her so much that it hurt. I made a decision and I asked her:

"Tell me about your need to be in control – to be the boss?"

"What can I say? I need to be in charge."

"Are we talking BDSM type stuff? Whips, chains, ball gags, handcuffs and stuff like that?"

"No, I just have to be in charge."

"Give me some examples."

She thought for a minute and said, "With the last guy he wanted to go to his apartment and I said no. I told him that I wouldn't feel comfortable at his apartment or taking him to my place so I told him we would go to the Fleetwood. I didn't suggest the Fleetwood or ask him if the Fleetwood would be okay, I just told him that we were going to the Fleetwood. Why the Fleetwood? I've no idea. Telling him what we are going to do was the point. The next night he wanted to go to The Stockman for dinner and I said no, we were going to Angelo's. Again, it was all about making him do what I wanted. It did not matter what he wanted I always wanted the opposite and I always got my way. It was like you put it – my way or the highway – and he went along with it every time."

"It sounds like you had the perfect man so why didn't you keep him?"

"Because I didn't love him. All I wanted was to boss him around."

"Do you need to love someone to boss them around? As long as you could push him around weren't you getting what you wanted?"

"Up to a point, yes."

"And that point was?"

"It's the flaw in the whole thing. I want to be the boss, I want to make him do what I want, but at the same time I was disgusted with him because he was spineless. He went along with everything I told him to do just because he wanted to get into my pants."

"Well it worked. He did get into your pants."

"Yes he did, but only because I wanted to boss him some more. He wanted a blow job and I told him I didn't do that."

"You do it all the time with me."

"Haven't you been listening to me, Rob? It isn't about what I like or do; it is all about what I can do to the guy. He wants head and I say no. He says he doesn't like to eat pussy, I say get down there and start munching or get out. It was all about me, Rob; all about me and what I wanted. I need that, Rob. I need to be able to push like that sometimes and I can do it to guys like the ones I've dated since I met you because I don't love them. I don't care about them in the least."

"Have any of them ever said, "No, I think we will do it this way?""

"None of them ever have."

"What would have happened if they would have?"

"I would have walked away from them. That is why we can't get married right now, Rob. Sooner or later I would try to boss you around and I know you well enough to know that you wouldn't put up with it and then I'd have a fit and it would go down hill from there."

"You are probably right about that, Maeve."

"So we can go back to the way we were?"

"No, Maeve, I don't think so. I'm not willing to be part-time."

She stood up and slowly undressed and then she cupped her tits in her hands and said;

"Are you telling me that you don't want this?"

"Of course I won't say that, but I am telling you that tonight is the last time. Next time you show up I won't let you in and you can take that to the bank."

"We will just see about that," she said and then she said, "Show me to the bedroom, lover."

It was another exhausting night.

She was waiting for me when I got home from work the next day and she was smiling until I closed the door in her face. The next three nights in a row she showed up and I wouldn't let her in my apartment. I didn't see her for a week and then one night she was sitting on the steps outside my apartment door waiting for me. She stood up as I approached and said:

"Okay, Rob, you win. Set a date."

\*\*\*

Maeve had no living relatives and all I had was a few aunts and uncles and my cousin George so we decided on a simple civil ceremony. Maeve knew a judge and arranged for him to perform the ceremony. A week before the wedding Maeve asked me to meet her for lunch. When I got to the restaurant she was already there and had ordered for the both of us. We made small talk as we ate and when we were done she asked me to come back to her office with her. She said she had someone she wanted me to meet.

When we entered the building the security guard waved her over and pointed out two men sitting in the waiting area. Maeve went over and talked with them for a minute and then she came back to me and we got on the elevator. The elevator stopped on ten which was the top floor of the building and Maeve led me down a hallway to a room that said Conference Room C on the door. We walked in the room and there was a man sitting at a long conference table with a pile of paperwork in front of him. He stood and greeted Maeve and then looked at me and said:

"Is this the lucky man?"

"Indeed he is. Rob, this is Milton Spaulding. Milton, meet Rob. Milton is my attorney."

I looked at her with some confusion on my face. "Your attorney?"

"Yes. Milton handles most of my affairs and he wanted this meeting."

"Most of your affairs?"

"It will all become clear in a second. Have a seat and let's get started."

"Started on what?"

Milton looked at me surprised. "The paper work, of course."

"Paper work? What paper work?"

Milton slid a folder over to me and said, "If you will just sign on the last page on the line provided," and he handed me a pen.

"Sign what?"

"The pre-nuptial agreement."

"A pre-nup? Why in the hell do we need a pre-nup?"

"It spells out the duties of both parties in the case of a break up of the marriage."

"I know what a pre-nup is. The question was why in the hell do we need a pre-nup. We aren't movie stars or anything like that. Why in the hell do a sales manager and an advertising agency secretary need a prenuptial agreement?"

"An advertising agency secretary?" Milton said and he and Maeve exchanged a look.

"He doesn't know," Maeve said.

Milton turned to me and said. "Miss Billings doesn't work for the agency, she owns it. The reason for the prenuptial agreement is that Miss Billings has a net worth close to sixteen million."

I have no idea what my facial expression looked like when I heard that, but if it were physically possible my jaw would have hit the floor. "Sixteen mil-" I muttered to myself and then I looked at Maeve and said:

"How much other shit are you hiding from me, Maeve. How many other secrets are you keeping from me? First there was the domineering shit and now this."

I pushed the folder back across the table to Milton. "No need for a pre-nup, Mr. Spaulding, because there isn't going to be a marriage."

I stood up and walked out of the conference room. The suddenness of my departure caught Maeve by surprise and I was almost to the elevator before she came running down the hall yelling:

"Where are you going, Rob? Wait, Rob, wait."

The elevator was still on the floor and the door opened as soon as I pushed the button. I stepped on and pushed the button for the lobby and the door closed as Maeve ran up, crying out:

"Wait, Rob. Please, Rob, don't go."

Just before the door closed I said, "Goodbye, Maeve."

When I reached the lobby and the elevator door opened I found the security guard standing there.

"I'm sorry, sir, but I've been instructed to hold you here until Miss Billings can get here."

"You certainly will be sorry if you get in my way."

I started to walk by him and he put out an arm to stop me and I kneed him in the balls and then walked by his bent over form. Once outside the building I called my secretary and told her I would be visiting customers and wouldn't be back to the office and then I turned my cell phone off and headed for the Extra Point.

About halfway there I decided against going. I didn't need any more drinking, I didn't feel like shooting pool and I damned sure didn't need to hear George tell me "I told you so." I drove out to Steven's Point and looked out over the lake and just stared at the geese and ducks with my mind a blank before getting myself together and going on home. I was not surprised to see Maeve's Jeep Cherokee in the parking lot and for a second or so I debated pulling back out of the lot and going to the Extra Point anyway. But then I decided to just get it over with.

She was not in the living room when I entered the apartment and that told me that she would probably be in the bedroom and no doubt naked so she could cloud my mind. I wasn't going to play that game. I went into the kitchen, got a beer from the fridge and sat down at the kitchen table. I was on my second beer when she came into the kitchen wearing my bathrobe. I didn't say a word; just looked at her and sipped my beer.

She stood there and watched me for several seconds and then she got herself a beer and sat down across from me. She took a pull on her beer and then said:

"Why didn't you wait when I asked you to?"

"Why and to what purpose? So you could feed me some more bullshit?"

"I never fed you any bullshit."

"No? What about letting me think you worked for an advertising agency?"

"That wasn't a lie. I do work there. Okay, so I didn't tell you the agency was mine. So what? I still work there."

"You are splitting hairs, Maeve, and you know it. Everything I know about you, everything you have led me to believe is a lie. The way you dress, the way you live, a two bedroom condo in Woods Park, a two-year-old Jeep Cherokee, all of it designed to make me think you are someone you aren't."

"I didn't do anything to mislead you, Rob. I drive a Jeep because I can throw my sleeping bag and camping gear in the back, put it in four wheel drive and go where I want. And why a two-year-old one when I could have the latest and greatest from Detroit? Have you seen the bangs and scratches on that car? I go to some pretty rough places with that Cherokee. Why should I waste good money on a new one just to beat it up?

"I live in a two bedroom condo because it suits me. I can only sleep in one bedroom at a time. I have an extra bedroom for company and I don't need any more than that. Where in the hell is it written that if somebody has money they have to spend it on things they don't need? Will a BMW, a Lexus or a Mercedes do a better job of hauling my camping gear? What good would having a five bedroom mansion do me? It would be one more thing to worry about. I'd have to hire a caretaker to take care of the grounds because I sure wouldn't. The same with the inside of the place. I'd have to hire a maid and God only knows what else. No thank you."

"You are still splitting hairs here, Maeve. You still hid things from me. The ownership of your agency, your money and who knows what else."

"Do you have any idea of how often men have tried to become "The love of my life" when they found out what I have? Do you have any idea of what it is like having to always wonder whether the man is really after you and not your money? My knowing that you didn't know is what allowed us to build the relationship we have."

"From your side maybe."

"What does that mean?"

"What that means is that what made our relationship possible was my being able to get by your "dates" while we were together, but we don't have a relationship any more. What took place in your conference room today ended it. I meant what I told your lawyer. There isn't going to be a marriage."

"That isn't fair, Rob."

"Was it fair to me to spring your surprise on me today. To have me walk into that conference room and then hit me with what you hit me with? Don't you think that since you had made up your mind that I didn't know what you had that you could have prepared me for Milton?"

"I thought you would be pleasantly surprised."

"Well I was surprised, but it wasn't very pleasant."

"You are over reacting here, Rob."

"Am I? What's tomorrow?"

"Thursday."

"And what was supposed to be special about this particular Thursday? We were going to shop for wedding rings. We don't even have the wedding rings yet, Maeve, and this afternoon you and your lawyer were already planning out what we will do in the divorce."

"That's not fair, Rob. Pre-nups are standard for people in my position."

"Well they aren't standard for people in my position and the last thing in the world I expected was to be hit with one out of left field. You need to put your clothes on and leave, Maeve."

"You don't mean that, Rob, you can't mean that."

"I'm sorry, Maeve, I can and I do. You have too many secrets, Maeve, and my capacity for surprises is limited. Your need to push men around and your sudden wealth were quite enough for me. Get dressed and go find some submissive guy and do your thing, but leave, Maeve, just leave. Put your key on the table and go."

Watching her walk out the door was one of the hardest things I'd ever had to do, but it had to be done. The Maeve I thought I knew did not exist.

# Chapter 2

It was hard to put Maeve out of my mind. Her scent was still on the bed. I washed the pillow covers, but her scent still lingered on the pillows themselves. Likewise the mattress. I kept finding things of hers that got left behind. A hairpin here, the button from a blouse there, a lipstick that had somehow rolled under the couch.

Maeve called me two or three times a day and I finally had to get an unlisted number for the home phone and a new cell phone number. She called me at work, but I had already bribed Donna to handle that. A couple of times when I came home from work she was waiting in the parking lot for me and as soon as I saw her I pulled out of the lot and found a sports bar where I could kill time until she left.

Then there was a three week spell when she didn't call me or my work or show in my parking lot and I began to think that she had finally got the message that we were through and I could get on with my life.

Silly me.

It was ten in the morning and I had just finalized a deal that I had been working on for two months. Donna stuck her head in my office and told me that Matt, my boss, wanted to see me in his office. I walked down the hall to it and Charlotte, his secretary, told me to go right in. I walked into Matt's office to find him standing next to his desk and talking to…Maeve! Matt saw me and said:

"Here he is now. Come in, Rob, have a seat. I believe you already know Miss Billings."

Maeve looked at me and smiled as she said, "Good morning, Rob."

She winced when I said, "Good morning, Miss Billings."

"Rob, Miss Billings came to me with an advertising idea that I like and since she already knows you and you know the ins and outs of what we do, she has asked that you work with her on it. This is really going to help us, Rob, so give her what she needs. I've got a ton of things to do this morning so why don't you take Miss Billings…"

"Please call me Maeve."

"Why don't you take Maeve over to your office and she can fill you in."

Once in my office I asked, "What are you up to, Maeve?"

"Oh come on, Rob, you aren't dumb. You won't take my calls, you run when you see me, so I needed a way to get to you that you couldn't avoid. I made your boss an offer he couldn't refuse and told him that I would need to work with you on it."

"But why, Maeve. I made it clear that we are history."

"Not while we are both still alive, Rob. You are my man and that is all there is to it. I'll do whatever I have to do to get you and keep you."

"Nothing has changed, Maeve. You know my feelings and they have not changed."

"No more secrets, Rob. You ask and I'll tell you whatever you want to know. I won't hide anything from you. And no pre-nup. What I have is yours and with no strings attached. All I want is you, Rob."

"I don't think so, Maeve. Now what is this thing you have sold Matt on and what do I need to do?"

"Give it up, Rob. There is no way that we can spend several hours a day together that I won't get to you. Why prolong it?"

Prolong it I did – for all of three weeks. But she was right. There was no way I could be constantly in her presence several hours a day and stay away from her. Slowly, but surely she pulled me back and a date was set for the wedding.

My apartment was too small so I moved into Maeve's condo and then Maeve set out to spoil me rotten. I love golf so she bought a membership in a country club. She thought I needed something a little more substantial than a five-year-old Chevy pickup so I came home from work one day and found a Cadillac STS parked in my assigned parking space. I would have preferred something a little less ostentatious, but recognizing Maeve's need to be in charge, I smiled and thanked her.

Next she decided that the condo was too small for us and decided that it was time to get a house. We must have looked at a hundred – quite a few that I liked – but Maeve didn't think that the ones I liked were good enough.

"We are going to entertain a lot, honey, so we need something with a pool and a large patio area," is what she said, but (and I was well aware of it) what she meant is that "I'M picking out the house." What the hell did I care? I was going from an apartment to a house and the truth of the matter is that I wouldn't mind having a place with a pool.

She finally picked a 12000-square-foot five-bedroom with an in ground swimming pool, a huge patio and two tennis courts. It had an attached four car garage and sat on five acres. She looked around and then did what she once told me that she didn't want to have to do. She hired a groundskeeper to take care of the outside and signed a contract with Molly Maids to take care of the inside.

We went furniture shopping for the new house and while she did ask my opinion, she bought what she wanted. There were some disagreements along the way and when a time or two I insisted on something, she got "huffy" with me, but I ignored her and she liked that even less. But I knew going in that she had a controlling nature and for the most part I let her have her own way. I was not unmindful of the fact that giving in to her on everything could lead her to start believing I was "spineless" and I was never going to allow that to happen even if I had to fight tooth and nail over something.

\*\*\*

The first three years went by and we were happy together. Things went smoothly as long as I let Maeve do what she wanted. I would throw up an occasional roadblock just to keep things honest.

The "control" and "in charge" were always there. Planning a vacation I suggested Cancun, but she said no, that St. Thomas was where she wanted to go. The next time I wanted to cross the water to England and she decided on Vancouver. The third year we were going to take three weeks off and she asked me where I thought we should go. By then I knew the playbook so I decided to get sneaky on her. We each had a home office, hers downstairs off the dining room and mine in one of the extra bedrooms upstairs, and one day when she wasn't home I went into her office and snooped around. I saw literature and brochures for Australia and New Zealand and I knew if I said France or Spain she would say maybe next time, but that she would like to go to Australia and New Zealand. The next time she brought the subject up I said that I'd always had a hankering to see New Zealand.

"Maybe some other time, but this year I think we should go to England and maybe cross the channel and spend a couple of days in France." I KNEW she wanted Australia, but it HAD to be her decision not mine and I knew that as soon as I said I wanted to go to New Zealand there wasn't any way in hell she would go there.

Why did I put up with that kind of bullshit? Because I loved the silly bitch and if giving in to her made her happy so be it. And besides, it wasn't as if I really cared where we went as long as we went there together.

The fourth year is when it started to go bad although it took me a while before I realized it. It started with Maeve working late two or three nights a week. There was always a good reason. Trouble with this advertising campaign. Problems with that client needing late meetings to solve. Hey! Maeve was in the advertising business and it was what she had to do, right? It took a while to register on me that the nights Maeve worked late we never made love when we went to bed.

"Too tired, baby."

"Not tonight, honey, I'm whipped."

"Maybe tomorrow, sweetie; I've got a ripping headache."

"Not now, Rob; I really don't feel like it."

This after us rarely going a week without making love three, four and sometimes five times a week. Then other things happened. Phone calls and no one there when I answered or the sound of someone hanging up when they heard my voice. Maeve on the phone saying, "Got to go. Talk to you later," when I would walk into the room. She took showers as soon as she got home and she had never done that before.

A couple of times I had come home during the day and found that Maeve was home also – with a man and a different man each time. Both times I had seen her car in the driveway and I had called out as I came into the house and by the time I got to the kitchen the man was sitting at the table and Maeve was digging through the icebox. The story was that they had been to a meeting with a client and were on the way back to the office and decided to stop and have lunch rather than returning to the office and then going out to lunch. Looking back on it now I can't believe how stupid I was. In my defense I can only say that I was in love and love can make you blind to some things.

Why would I think she was cheating on me? Hadn't she busted her ass to get me? Hadn't she done everything including almost crawling to get me back after I split from her?

The beginning of the end came about by a fluke. Maeve called me and told me that she was working another late night. Ten minutes after she called the out of town client I was working with asked me to join him for dinner. The restaurant he wanted to go to was on the other side of town – a side of town I rarely visited. It turned out that the reason he wanted to go there was that his daughter worked there as a waitress while attending college.

We drove over, met his daughter and had dinner. After dinner he wanted to go to the lounge across the street and have a drink or two. The place was pretty dark inside except for the dance floor area. Fred and I took a corner booth in one of the back corners. I was halfway through my first drink when Fred said:

"Now there is one lucky son of a bitch."

I turned to see what he was looking at and saw Maeve dancing with some guy. She did look spectacular. She and the guy she was dancing with were pressed pretty tight together and the guy had both hands on her ass and was pulling her into him as he ground his dick into her leg.

Some other guy might have gotten up and stormed out onto the dance floor and kicked some ass and then told his wife what he thought of her, but I didn't do that. For one thing, deep down inside of me somewhere I think I always expected that Maeve and I were not destined for the long haul. I suppose it went back to the "dates" she went on when we were going together and spending most of our nights together. I did know that I was disappointed. I also knew that it was over between Maeve and me. There wasn't any story she could tell me that I would buy. If she had been sitting there having a drink, I might have bought that she was having a drink with a client much as I was, but no client is going to have both hands on your ass and grind his cock into you.

The song ended and Maeve and the man kissed and moved off the dance floor and to a booth where two other men were sitting. I finished my drink and told Fred that I needed to be going and he told me he was going to be spending the night with his daughter so I said my goodbyes and left. I headed on home and as I drove I started mentally making lists of what I needed to do. I was in bed when Maeve got home. She showered before coming to bed and when she got in bed she snuggled up to me and I pretended to be asleep.

In the morning I was up and gone before Maeve got up. When I got to work I called an apartment finding service and told them what I wanted. At lunch time I hit a couple of used car lots and found a two year old Chevy crew cab with a long bed and put a deposit on it. Just before quitting time I called Maeve and told her I would be working late and then made sure that I didn't go home until after I knew she would have gone to bed.

For the next two weeks I avoided Maeve as much as possible. The apartment finding service had found several places that met my criteria and I went and looked at them. I chose one and put a deposit on it and then I got out the Yellow Pages and found an attorney close to the office and I called and made an appointment.

By the time I had everything in place three weeks had gone by since I had seen Maeve at the Purple Mushroom. She was a little perturbed with me because I had been avoiding her and we hadn't had sex in three weeks, but I was able to sell her the story that we were working at a very lucrative contract at work and it was causing me to work extremely late hours and I was dead tired when I got home.

"You know how it is, Maeve. Look at all the late nights you have been putting in working on campaigns and deals."

There wasn't much she could say to that.

Then the day came when my attorney told me the divorce papers were ready to be served and I set it up to have Maeve served at her office. The grounds were Irreconcilable Differences. I couldn't go for Adultery because I had no proof, but it didn't matter since all I wanted was out of the marriage and any grounds that would get it done were all that I needed.

That night was another night when I called Maeve and told her that I would be working late again.

"But guess what? We finished up the paperwork today and this will be the last night I'll have to work late."

I hit The Extra Point and shot some pool until I thought Maeve would be in bed and then I went home. Maeve wasn't there when I got there. I went into my home office and made sure that I had everything I wanted all boxed and ready to go. I had already lined up George to help me load what I wanted into my truck the next day. I took one last look around and then I headed for the bedroom. I had no idea where Maeve was – or with who – but I wanted to be in bed and pretending to be asleep when she got there.

I was on my way up to the bedroom when Maeve came in. She wasn't alone.

"Rob, this is Jack. Jack wants me to be his fuck-toy and I didn't think you would mind. After all, you haven't had anything to do with me for almost a month now. Jack thought you might be a little upset, but I told him that if you didn't like it you could leave."

I turned to the guy and smiled as I said, "No problem, Jack. Obviously she wants to be your fuck-toy or she wouldn't have brought you home with her. The secret to a good marriage, Jack, is to let your wife do whatever it is that makes her happy. Matter of fact to make things easier on all concerned I'll move my things to one of the other bedrooms and let you have the master bedroom. Give me just a minute and I'll be out of your way."

As I turned to walk away, I saw the shock on Maeve's face. I went to the bedroom and got my tooth brush and shaving gear and took them to the bedroom down the hall, locked the door behind me and got into bed. There was a smile on my face because Maeve had just made things so much easier for me.

Twenty minutes after I went to bed someone tried to come into the room, but the door was locked. There was a knock on the door and I ignored it. Another couple of knocks that I also ignored and then Maeve called out:

"Rob? Unlock the door, Rob. Open the door, Rob; we need to talk."

I just laid there and ignored her. She tried for ten minutes, but I never responded. Finally she gave up and said:

"I'll talk to you in the morning."

In the morning I was up and out of the house before Maeve was even awake. I drove over and picked up George and we went to breakfast. Then we drove over to the parking lot at work and picked up the Chevy from where it had been parked since I bought it. Then George drove the Caddy and followed me back to the house. Maeve was gone, either to work or to take Jack back to where she had found him, and George and I started to load the truck. We were loaded in a little under an hour. I tossed my wedding ring and the keys to the Caddy on the kitchen table and then we drove over to my new apartment and started moving me in.

We hadn't been there ten minutes when my cell beeped. It was Maeve.

"I called you at work and they told me you took the day off. Where are you?"

"Moving into my new apartment."

"What! Why in the world are you doing that?"

"Think about it for a bit, Maeve. Maybe it will come to you."

I disconnected and then turned off the phone. We got everything moved in and I ran George home and then I went back to settle into my new digs. I smiled when the alarm built into my wrist watch went off at eleven. That was the time we had set it up for Maeve to be served with the divorce papers. For a moment or so I flirted with the idea of turning my cell back on so I could take Maeve's call, but then decided to forego the pleasure.

I had taken the whole week off from work so if I left my cell off it would be five days before Maeve could reach me. A private detective wouldn't help her this time – at least not until I went back to work and he could follow me home. I spent those five days at a cabin I rented on Lake Owens and then Monday I returned to work. There was a stack of messages three inches high from Maeve and I tossed them into the trash. I bribed Donna again to keep Maeve from being put through to me on the phone and then I went and had a little talk with Matt. I told him the situation and that I did not care how good a deal Maeve might offer him, I would have nothing to do with her.

I managed to avoid Maeve for almost a month and then she played the only card she had. My attorney called me and said her attorney had called and wanted a meeting. I guess I could have just said:

"Meeting? We don't need no stinking meting!"

But I wanted the thing to be over with so I decided not to do anything that would slow things down and I said I would be there.

Milton and Maeve were already sitting at the table in the conference room with my attorney when I walked into the room. Maeve started to get up, but Milton pulled her back down. Milton scowled at me when I sat down and muttered:

"I knew – just knew – there needed to be a pre-nup as soon as I saw you."

I laughed and then asked, "Are you a real lawyer, Milton? I mean have you been admitted to the bar and all that?"

Milton started to say something, but I continued. "A real lawyer would at least be familiar with the paper work his client had been served with. No need for a pre-nup, Milton, because the only thing I asked for was my freedom. I even gave her back the Cadillac she bought me. Just out, Milton; that's all I asked for was out."

I leaned back and faced Milton and Maeve and said, "Now what in the hell is this meeting about?"

Maeve spoke up and said, "I don't want out, Rob. I do not want a divorce and getting you to this meeting seemed to be the only way I could get face to face with you and talk."

"We have nothing to talk about, Maeve. We are done, toast, through, finished."

"Why, Rob? Why are you doing this?"

"Does the name Jack ring a bell?"

"Bullshit, Rob. You were out of the house and moving into a new apartment the next morning. You couldn't have found a place and made arrangements that quick. It all had to be in place before Jack."

"Jack wasn't the first one, Maeve, and we both know it. Now, if we have nothing more to discuss I have other things to do with my time."

Maeve then asked the two attorneys if she might have a few moments in private with me. My attorney looked at me and I shrugged and he and Milton got up and left the room. As soon as the door closed behind them Maeve said:

"There were no others, Rob. There wasn't even a Jack."

"I know better, Maeve. I personally saw you in action with one of your boyfriends."

"He wasn't my boyfriend, Rob; he is one of my account reps and we were at the Purple Mushroom wining and dining a client. I saw you come in and I asked Mack to help me tweak your nose a bit."

"You may have seen me, Maeve, but I'm betting that it wasn't until after I saw you rubbing crotches with that guy. And I don't believe he was the first. If he was the first I'll bet it had been going on for some time before that night."

"That's not true, Rob. There has never been anyone but you."

"I don't believe that, Maeve."

"Why don't you believe it? It is true."

"Is it, Maeve? Then explain a few things to me," and I laid out all the signs that pointed to her cheating – besides the night at the Purple Mushroom and the night she brought Jack home with her.

She looked down at the table and then said, "I swear to God, Rob, there has never been anyone else."

I just sat there and looked at her.

"Honest, Rob; no one but you. Looking at it now I can see that it was stupid. I wish I could take it back, but I can't."

"Take what back, Maeve?"

"It goes back to my controlling nature, Rob. I let it get the best of me. You never said no to me, Rob. You always gave in when I wanted something. I got to wondering if you had any limits – a point where you would push back. But you never did push back. It didn't matter what I did, you went along with it so I got the bright idea of trying to find something that you would have to get riled up over so I pretended that I was having an affair. I kept doing all the things that I thought would make you suspicious and demand to know what was going on, but you never did anything. Phony phone calls and you never said a word. Not coming home until late and then taking a shower drew no comment. Nothing I did got a rise out of you.

"I began thinking that you didn't care because you really didn't love me. I started thinking that your walking out of the meeting where Milton brought up the pre-nuptial agreement was a ploy. You knew I'd come after you so you played 'hard-to-get' until I said okay, no pre-nup. I was in that doubting frame of mind the night I saw you come into the Purple Mushroom and I decided to give you something you couldn't ignore. I asked Mack to help me play a joke on you and when you didn't come out onto the dance floor I was sick. I knew then that you didn't care. I just knew that when I got home that night you would dump on me. You didn't say a thing or do a thing.

"But I finally got a reaction. It wasn't the one I wanted, but I got a reaction. You ignored me. The more you ignored me the more pissed off I got and the madder I got the more I wanted to do something that would rock you and that is where Jack came in. When I hit you with Jack you took it calmly, smiled and said have fun and walked away. It broke my heart. It proved that I meant nothing to you. I sent Jack on his way and went to the bedroom you were in to have it out with you once and for all, but you wouldn't let me in or talk to me and the next morning you were gone.

"I swear to you, Rob, there was never anyone else."

"Of course there was, Maeve. There was the other you."

"The other me?"

"Yes, Maeve, there was the loving wife who spoiled me rotten and then there was the scheming, controlling bitch that just had to play her sick games. It has been there all along. The woman who loved me and the slut that had to walk away every once in a while on "dates." Apparently that never stopped. I don't know at what point in our marriage you started going on your "dates" again and I don't care. You games backfired and bit you on the ass, Maeve.

"I saw all the signs that pointed to cheating and I ignored them because they must have been innocent coincidences. They had to have been because I just knew that you had to love me as much as I loved you. I saw the signs but I ignored them because I loved you too much to believe they could be true. Then came the Purple Mushroom and I realized that they must have been true after all.

"I never pushed back at you, Maeve, because I loved you and I wanted you to be happy. Being in charge – being in control – seemed to keep you happy so I let things go. Well, Maeve, you wanted to find out if I had limits and now you know that I do have them and you found them and pushed me past them. I hope you are happy now that you know where they are."

"So you will come home?"

"No, Maeve, I'm out and I'm staying out. I told you once before that I had a limited capacity for surprises. You have passed that limit."

"Doesn't it matter to you that I love you?"

"Of course it matters, Maeve, but I'm not going to go through this shit every time you get a wild hair up your ass."

"It will never happen again, Rob. I swear to God it will never happen again."

"You kind of promised me something like that once before and we both remember how that turned out. No more surprises you said, but here we are. Two years, five years or maybe ten years from now I don't want to go through this again. Best we end it right now and move on."

"I don't want a divorce, Rob."

"I didn't want a cheating wife either. I listened to your story and maybe some or even all of it might be true, but in the back of my mind I will always wonder if your story was true or made up to suit the occasion. Little things would jump out at me. Things like you saying that at the Purple Mushroom you finally realized that I didn't care. If you believed I didn't care and you didn't do anything that night why did you take a shower when you got home and before you got in bed?

"I will always suspect that you did cheat and I won't live like that. I'll always see Mack and you grinding into each other and then that long hot kiss when the song ended. I will always see the smirk on Jack's face as you said you were going to be his fuck-toy. It is over, Maeve."

"I won't give you a divorce, Rob. I'll use every cent that I have to fight it."

"You can stop it, Maeve. You have enough money that you can pay Milton to file papers and do whatever lawyers do for years and years and I won't be able to pay my attorney to fight you. But it won't matter, Maeve, because I'm gone and I'm not coming back. Get used to it, Maeve; as a couple we are history and you have no one to blame but yourself."

\*\*\*

Maeve did use her money to keep Milton busy filing motions and briefs and whatever. I paid off my lawyer and got on with my life. It has been over two years now and Maeve and I are still legally married and once or twice a month she will call me and ask me if I have come to my senses yet and if I'm ready to come home. I never give her an answer other than to just hang up.

I've had a lot of girlfriends during that period - a couple have even moved in and lived with me for a while – at least until they find out that marriage is not in the cards for us and then they slowly drift away. I suppose it is a good thing because I'm not sure that I'll ever want to get married again. I figure that sooner or later Maeve will though and when that happens she can take care of the divorce.

Maybe just to be spiteful I'll fight it.


## ~~The End~~

**\*Here is a sample from another story you may enjoy!\***

# JUST PLAIN BOB

# BUYING MY WIFE

## Adult Erotica

The first thing I did when I got back to my office was get out the Yellow Pages and turn to Investigators and Investigative Services. There were three within two blocks of my office and the first two I called couldn't see me for three or four days but the third one said, "Come on down." As I walked the two blocks to Acme Investigative Services I tried to think of what Hargrove must have been smoking. There was no way that Abby could be having an affair with him let alone be planning on marrying him. We were too happy together. We had a great relationship, but at the same time I couldn't help but feel that something made Hargrove approach me and the best way to find out what it was was to put someone on the case to check things out. Maybe Abby was just a good friend and he misunderstood her feelings. For my own peace of mind I needed to find out what was going on.

I met with Mr. Owen Paulson and filled him in on my meeting with Hargrove. I told him that I seriously doubted that my wife was being unfaithful, but I did need to know what Hargrove was up to. The only times Abby was out of the house were for her Tuesday night book club and discussion group, her Thursday night bridge club meeting and her Saturday morning beauty shop appointment to have her hair done while I played golf with three of my friends. I gave Paulson all the information he asked for regarding Abby and then I gave him a check to get him started. Since it was a Wednesday he told me they would put an operative on Abby Thursday morning when she left the house to go to work and then watch her until the following Tuesday. He told me I could stop by or call him Wednesday for a report.

As I walked back to my office I spent more time trying to figure out what Hargrove was really after. I had absolutely no doubt about Abby's love for me, but I could not figure out for the life of me what Hargrove's angle was.

Abby usually beat me home and when I got home that night she was in the kitchen fixing dinner. She stopped what she was doing, came to me and put her arms around me and kissed me. Dinner and dishes out of the way we curled up on the couch to watch some TV and Abby moved in next to me, put her head on my shoulder and cuddled up next to me. This woman cheating on me? No way!

If you enjoyed this sample then look for **Buying My Wife**.

**Also by this Author:**

The Prodigal Family: The Abbotts

Watching My Shared Wife

The Waitress and the Runaway Husband

Baiting Mr. Little

Too Hot for Henry

Chuck's Fantasy

The Redhead's Desires

Rescued at Riley's

His Every Fantasy

Open Mike Night

Pursuit for Revenge

Why Does He Do That?

Halloween & Drugs

Tracey

When Rob Met Kari

Becoming a Shared Wife, Vol. 1 –
(Wife Sharing and Other Adventures)

Becoming a Shared Wife, Vol. 2 –
(Hazardous Wives)

Becoming a Shared Wife, Vol. 3 –
(Wives Who Stray)

Erotica Short Stories, Vol. 8 –

(Wild Urges)

Erotica Short Stories, Vol. 9 –

(Horny)

Erotica Short Stories, Vol. 10 –

(Stuffed Hard)

Erotica Short Stories, Vol. 11 –

(9 Shades of Sex)

Erotica Short Stories, Vol. 12 –

(Doing What She Does Best)

Erotica Short Stories, Vol. 13 –

(Hottest Nights)

A Weird One

Blackmailed MILF

Filthy Steps With My…

The Biggest She's Ever Had

Sharing Penny

Hardest Nights

My Woman's Dirty Secrets

She Makes Me...

She Needs More

My Wife's Inferno

Dirty Love

Hot & Tight

Her Illicit Adventures

What I Want To Do To Her

Too Fun To Give Up

Creamed

Stepping Out

Hottest Wife

Naughty Wives

Deepest and Darkest

More Than She Can Take

Jennifer's Toes

The More The Sexier

Spice Up

Cyndi

Naughty And Nice

House Of Lovers

Hungry For More

Sweet Revenge

Turning Mommies Wild: The Carriage Tales

Bought And Used

Get Me Off

The Gambler

Gail's Price

## Family Affair

## Buying My Wife

**You may also like the books by these authors:**

Wild Erotic Romance

# Risky Sideline

Rhys Lysander

It was a Saturday evening, just after sunset, when she stepped into the waiting car. By request, she had straightened her normally somewhat curly hair, and had it pulled back into a long pony tail. Some hair extensions helped with the look. Opening the bag waiting on the rear seat beside her she found a pair of mid calf leather boots, a pair of very short khaki shorts, a black web belt, a khaki backpack, two holsters with straps labeled for her 'right and left thighs,' two solid plastic (and fake) HK semi-automatic pistols, and a way to small teal sports bra. When she saw the top she laughed aloud—she'd never envisioned herself playing Lara Croft.

'Lara' was fully dressed when the car stopped. She exited and made her way to the faintly lit doorway and down the stairs concealed beyond. The stairwell was lit by candles spaced every few feet, and was warm and humid. Her boots were nearly silent as she descended into the darkness of the basement. Arriving on the last stair, she paused to let her eyes adjust to the darkness. The basement had been transformed into an ancient chamber. No doubt a treasure, hinted at in the dossier, was hidden within. Sculptures and intricate relief carvings lined the walls. Torches were well placed to fully illuminate the room. Lara pulled her pistols and slowly crept around the room to examine everything.

When she finished some twenty minutes later there were two things that caught her attention and were worthy of more study. First was the altar at the far side of the room, opposite the entrance. When she had knelt beside it she noticed there were odd depressions not only in the top of the altar, but in the floor at its base. The altar was lower than she expected, but yet too high to be used if she was kneeling. Second was a sort of totem pole. It was not free standing, but a column that seemed to be part of the wall itself, with half of it exposed and the other half behind the wall. Four feet off the floor were a pair of carvings that looked to be hand holds. The column was intricately carved with nude figures of both men and women. A life size male figure with an impressive cock was centered between the hand hold carvings. It seemed rather obvious what she was supposed to do. Seeing no threats, she holstered her HKs and approached the column.

Lara reached to the right and left and ran her hands over the carvings. Unlike the column, which had the texture of stone, the hand hold carvings felt like hardwood and were very, very smooth. She enjoyed the tactile sensation of running her hands over them. Touching both of them her face was not even an inch from the heavy prick belonging to the stone man on the column. Gently she ran the pads of her fingers over the handles, feeling for any differences. Each index finger encountered a discontinuity that had to be a button. Taking a deep breath, she pressed them together.

For a moment, she wondered if nothing would happen, and then something clamped hard across her wrists, locking them in place. The sound of shifting sand and grating stone found her ears, and the panel in front of her started to lower. At first she could not tell if the panel with the cock was moving or she was, but then she realized her head was not moving relative to the rest of the column. As the panel descended, a hole opened up in the column and slowly, a very hard, very human cock poked out of the hole and moved steadily toward her. Lara leaned her head back, but starting only an inch from the column, she could not move very far. Hoping it held the key to unlocking the treasure, Lara relented and took the large phallus in her mouth. In moments enough length was protruding from the column and into her mouth and across her tongue that even when she tried to pull back she could not lean back far enough to disengage.

As the tomb raider started to rub the underside of the cock holding her head in place, she heard another scraping sound below her. She moved her legs around, trying to feel the column and learn what was happening, but without effect. Then, hearing shifting stone once more, her feet were slowly moved apart. When she tried to pull them together, they were blocked. The sound of a blade clearing a stone sheath rang in the silence. Her blood pulsed in her ears and she licked and sucked strongly on the cock in her mouth. She felt the blade as it pressed against her abdomen. Bobbing her head and sucking, she tried to assuage the spirit of the column. Relief gave way to trepidation as the pressure on her abdomen fled and she heard and felt the fabric of her shorts ripping.

The warm moist air blew across her pussy and she knew she was wet. Tightening her grip on the handholds, she pushed the intruding cock deep into her mouth and into her throat. Rubbing her tongue feverishly along the sensitive underside she sought to get it to release its load and soften it so she might break free. But even as she did, something impossibly smooth, wet and thick pressed against her nether lips. She tried to look down, but found she could not move her head enough to see anything. Her protestations and grunts totally ineffectual, the intruder, feeling as thick as her wrist, pushed steadily up into the empty channel that awaited it.

Pulling back from the cock in her mouth, Lara groaned as the largest thing ever to part her pussy lips sheathed itself inside her. Though it was only six inches inside her, the girth of it nearly took her breath away. Then, just as she got used to the intrusion, she felt the base of it come to rest against her opening. Unable to look down, she felt what seemed like a narrow saddle come to rest against her inner thighs as the thick dildo, or whatever it was, started to lift her up. Lara found she could support her weight on her tip toes for a few moments here and there, but whenever she slipped she was instantly impaled to the hilt on the giant phallus. The cock in her mouth seemed to enjoy her efforts, and its precum was readily flowing across her tongue.

What she seemed to not notice was that her frantic efforts to avoid fucking the thick phallus were, in fact, driving her to fuck it at an increasingly rapid pace. The movement also resulted in her mouth fucking the cock still lodged there, and the tandem events were having a pronounced effect on the bound tomb raider.

Subconsciously, Lara battled the cock in her mouth, trying to get it to spend, just as she struggled to keep her footing and stay off the impaling phallus in her pussy. At the same time, one effort failed and the other quickly succeeded.

As Lara's legs finally gave out, the feeling of surrender joined with the feeling of fullness and pressure against her overexcited clit combining to trigger a climax worthy of poets. At once her legs gave up all pretense of holding her away from the intruding prick, and her hips ground her clit against the saddle mount with a mind of their own. Lara, dazed with pleasure, sucked greedily on the cock in her mouth, bobbing her head and rubbing her tongue in a ravenous drive to get it to deliver its cargo.

Long delayed, her orgasm made her whole body shudder. Her hips, long kept from doing what they so eagerly sought to do, bucked and bucked, driving her clit into the saddle and forcing her to another peak. "Nnnnggghhh!!!" she grunted around the stiff rod in her mouth. And then, in the brief moment between peaks, she felt the cock stiffen on her tongue. "Mmmmmmm," she purred. The next instant the cock started to twitch. She thrust her head forward and put her nose against the stone, placing the jumping cock at the entrance of her throat. With her tongue along the underside, she felt the pulses start and then travel along her tongue. Fluid reached her senses and she swallowed eagerly, and reflexively. Again she moaned as several more pulses flowed into her mouth.

Greedily she swallowed every drop, barely tasting the column's spend yet fully enjoying the completion of her task. Even as she finally realized her weight was resting on her pussy, her feet took up her weight as the phallus slowly lowered and pulled out of her. "Unnngh," she groaned at the sudden feeling of emptiness. "Fuuuuck," she said slowly, realizing the column's cock had withdrawn from her mouth. Finding her hands free and the column returned to its earlier form, she sat down in a heap and laid her head back against it. "Do I even want to look at the altar?" she said to herself.

The well breasted tomb raider, briefly satiated by her encounter with the column, let her eyes close: the altar and the treasure, if there was any, could wait a little while for her to catch her breath. Moments after her eyes closed she fell asleep where she sat. She was awakened some time later by a loud grating sound. She stood as she blinked away her disorientation, oblivious to the fact her shorts were no longer with her. She put her hands on her guns. "Who's there?"

A voice called out of the darkness beyond, "Lara, is that you?"

"Alex? Is that you? What are you doing here?"

"Hoping to keep you from making a big mistake." He emerged from the newly revealed tunnel, which closed behind him before he could react. "I know you still want the treasure, but the price is too high."

Lara looked over him. She guessed his age to be mid to late twenties. He was quite average looking, with short blonde hair, but he was wearing a snug fitting brown t-shirt and looked quite cut. She wondered if he might be the man behind the column. She figured that was the case, as her dossier had not specified allowing two men to have her. Still, stranger things had happened. She did not have to lodge a complaint if she did not want to. She blew her bangs out of her face, continuing to stand with her feet slightly apart. He surprised her by not staring at her bare pussy. She crossed her arms under her breasts. He -did- look at them. Of course he was a breast man.

"Alex, it's nice that you are worried about me, but I know you." He looked at her quizzically. "If you are here then you must have some plan to steal the treasure and leave me here."

"Now Lara, why would I do that?"

"Because you're Alex."

He shrugged. "I concede the point." He wiggled a finger at her, "Nevertheless, I think the price is too high for you to pay."

She placed her hands on her hips and cocked them to one side. Then he did steal a look at her crotch. She noticed a bulge in his pants. A very respectable bulge. "Uh huh. Shall we have a look at the altar together then?"

He held forth a hand and gestured for her to lead the way.

The altar was too high to be used by a kneeling penitent, and yet lower than would be useful for someone standing. The altar was joined to the wall, yet was wide enough to prevent touching the wall if you tried to reach it. There were depressions in the surface, and in the edge, and standing against it, it did not take her long to realize what was supposed to happen. She turned and faced Alex. "So, I gather I'm just supposed to bend over, put my breasts on the altar and wait for something to happen?"

Alex looked only slightly dumbfounded...before he grinned. "That's what I meant. Lara, my read of the scrolls of Te-Ra is that the treasure will only be released to one who is at once pure and not pure."

"And just how am I supposed to be pure and not pure?"

Now he was grinning completely. "Well, as I see it, a virgin who has sex for the first time at the altar would fit the meaning of the scrolls."

"Uh huh. I think you should know me well enough to know that I'm not a virgin."

"What I think is that you talk a good game, but though you may have fooled around quite a bit you haven't ever let anyone take your virginity."

She smirked. "You should have been here twenty minutes ago."

"Why? Was there a man in here?"

Lara recalled that while it had undoubtedly been a flesh and blood cock, and then cum, in her mouth, it had not been a live cock inside her pussy. "Yes, but just how might this magic interpret 'virgin'."

He shrugged. "I would have to guess in the Bill Clinton definition."

"Meaning anything other than penis in vagina is not sex." She noted his bulge was a bit bigger.

He tried to be serious. "I would say so. The magic would be specific, not interested in nuance, deception or semantics."

She looked at him suspiciously. "So, what, I'm just supposed to bend over and let you fuck me?"

He shook his head. "No, of course not. You should take your top off, bend over, put your breasts on the altar and ask me to fuck you."

She laughed out loud despite herself. "Well, I have to hand it to you Alex, that's the most direct pick up line anyone has ever dared use on me. Do you believe this is going to work and get us the treasure?"

He smiled, genuinely. "I have to admit, I'm not sure about the treasure, but I am sure that the door is only going to open if there is a sacrifice on the altar."

"That sounds extreme."

"Poor choice of words. I simply meant that you sacrifice your virginity, and then we get out."

A mischievous thought crossed her mind and she grinned at him. "I have an idea. What if I take your virginity."

Alex was flummoxed. "Wha, what?"


If you enjoyed this sample then look for **Risky Sideline.**

# Playing BY THE Rules

MMFF EXHIBITIONISM EROTICA

## LEON RANDALL

The doorway was open enough for sound to travel, although not especially well; and as Jan and I busied ourselves for bed, we could hear our friends doing likewise on their side. They talked quietly with each other and we could catch the odd word. Soon enough both couples were settling down and the getting-ready-for-bed noises faded away as the lights went out on both sides. I think it was Jan who called out "Good night, folks. Sleep well," which drew a similar response from Eva, and silence and darkness settled.

I knew Jan was tired as well. We sleep naked, and she was snuggling up to me in a spoon-type position, her buttocks comfortably nestled against my crotch and thighs, which is how we usually drift off when the room is cool, as it was here. It was crossing my mind whether Mr. Willy should make a nudging appearance in the bed but, truth to tell, I was feeling weary myself by now so I decided to let the idea pass. There was always morning to look forward to.

About a minute later, though a bit muffled by the distance from their room, I clearly heard Russell's voice. "Hey Leon. The room service here is great. They've put a woman in my bed."

This brought me quickly back up from my drift into sleep. Smiling to myself, I lifted my head from the pillow and spoke towards the ajar doorway. "Wow. Did you pay extra?"

His reply wafted through the doorway. "No, it must be part of the deal. Didn't you get one?"

I cast about for something witty to say in response. "Just a minute. I'll check." I paused theatrically for a second before adding, "Well, I'll be darned. I've got one too!"

While this exchange had been going on, I had propped myself up on an elbow and Jan had come back to more wakefulness, rolling onto her back. In the combined glow from around the window coverings and the digital clock, I could see her looking up at me. I whispered to her, "Seems that someone's not tired." Then, assuming that Jan was OK with me carrying on this exchange, I projected my voice towards the doorway again. "What a great place. I should come here more often."

Russell responded, dripping with double meaning. "I haven't come here at all yet, but I live in hope." At this, I thought I heard a quiet feminine giggle from their room.

Keep in mind that I was tired, had enjoyed a few drinks, and wasn't firing in ultra-quick mode, so I didn't have a clever response immediately on my lips. As I cast about for something clever to say, Russell's voice flowed again into our room. "What's yours like?" he asked.

Despite being tired, this was starting to be fun. As I contemplated what clever thing to say in response, I found myself without really thinking about it slipping my free hand up and down Jan as we lay there, as if I was actually trying to answer his question. My left hand had been resting on her tummy as this exchange started, but with a mind of its own, it wandered over her boobs in the seconds before my response. "It's dark," I said. "I can't really tell. But she's got curves." I paused, and then added, "Hey. I found bosoms."

Sounding not at all sleepy, Russell's voice came back, "You lucky devil. Let me check mine." There was a pause for a second or two, and a giggle again. "Yes, mine has those too. This is great!"

Warming to the dialogue, and straying my hand down over Jan's thighs and pubes, I found myself saying in to the gloom, "Does yours have a slit as well?"

Jan gave me a friendly (or, at least, I assumed it was) jab in the ribs with her elbow at this remark. Russell responded quickly. "Let me check." There was a short pause, then, "Yes. Yes she does. This just gets better and better."

I could hear a murmured conversation now, and a muffled giggle from their room. Then Russell's voice came to us again. "I've found a problem with mine. She talks. I'm being told to shut up and go to sleep." I thought for a moment then replied, "Try giving her something to suck on. That should stop her talking."

Jan whispered, "You're awful." She was fully awake now, and showed that she was warming to the amusing byplay we were part of by giving my Willy a couple of friendly twiddles as we lay there, waiting, not sure where this was going or what to say next.

A few moments later, Russell was speaking again. "You're a genius. Worked like a charm."

We could hear some whispers and more muffled giggles from their side, and then one or both of them was hamming it up with exaggerated, wet slurping sounds, lip-smacking and sucking noises. Whether or not they were actually doing anything sexual was impossible to say but, in any case, the play acting was very funny.

If you enjoyed this sample then look for **Playing By The Rules**.

# MFF Bisexual Threesome Romance

# She Made Him
# Do It

## Nicki Homewood

After a hundred metres or so they came to a pier that struck out from the riverside ten metres or so into the river itself. It was unlit and disappeared into the blackness of the river, the glare from the streetlights barely reaching the end of it. When they initially arrived it seemed very dark and forbidding, but their eyes quickly adjusted to the gloom.

Rob had an idea and took Natalya by the hand, leading her away from the footpath and right to the end of the pier. She walked up to the steel railings at the end and looked down at the black depths of the river running beneath their feet.

There were very few people walking along the footpath, and the lighting meant that even as they walked past the end of the pier, they would hardly be able to see anything of couple on the pier.

Rob stood behind Natalya and surrounded her, putting a hand onto the railing on either side of her. He pressed himself into her bum, feeling his erection grow in anticipation of what he was planning.

He moved his hands down to her dress and gently pulled it up until the hem was level with her waist. He calculated that her jacket was still hanging down in either side to protect her dignity to some degree but from the opposite bank she would be completely exposed.

He lowered his hand to her button and started to gently massage it, gratified that he could feel she was already aroused, her lips wet with her juices, demonstrably wanting him.

He decided that he would see if he could first give her an orgasm standing there on the pier, and turned his full attention to her oyster, playing with it with both fingers, moving them up and down with focused attention.

Natalya had been shocked when he had first pulled up her skirt; she knew in the back of her mind that her jacket made it difficult for anyone on their side of the river to see anything, but it did not alter the fact that she was standing in the centre of London with her entrance completely exposed to anyone on the river bank north of them.

Quickly though, the insistent movements of Rob's fingers seduced her body into arousal and acceptance. She tensed her legs, eager to feel the satisfaction of him finishing her.

When she finally came, it was with a light scream, only just audible to anyone walking along the footpath. For a moment they both relaxed, their breath quickening. Neither one of them was satisfied though, and immediately Rob unzipped his fly and pulled his pole free from its enclosure. He had been aroused to some degree for a long time, as Natalya had been wearing so little, but now was utterly ready.

"Do me," was the simple command that Natalya uttered at this point, both willing and desperate in its tone.

Needing no such invitation, Rob lifted the back of Natalya's jacket where it hung down over her bum. With his fingers he reached round and pulled her lips wide open, feeling the hard tip of his shaft ready to enter her.

Natalya shifted her pose a little, moving her feet slightly apart and leaning a bit forward onto the railings. Almost immediately she felt him slide swiftly up inside her, as once again she screamed out into the night.

"Do me hard," she insisted again, unnecessarily—even as she said the words, Rob had moved his hands down to her hips and was pulling himself deeper than ever into her.

They were both lost in the moment by this time, oblivious to their central London situation, oblivious to the other couple that was watching them from the bank just behind them.

Rob leaned forwards and placed his fingers back on Natalya's button, resuming his swift but gentle ministrations, sometimes touching the side of his shaft as it slipped in and out of her.

They were utterly shocked however when just a few metres away, two fellow revellers arrived next to them. Rob noticed them first and immediately stopped his movements, Natalya turned to see why and then also realised the proximity of the intruders. They both stood up straight, but Rob remained stock still, his heart racing, his length still firmly ensconced deep inside her.

Their minds raced—what should they do—was it better just to stay there until the other couple went, or to cut their losses and run? They remained transfixed until suddenly it became clearer what was going on.

The other couple was also involved in a deeply sexual adventure, her arms were around his shoulders and she was kissing him deeply and passionately. His hands were roaming all over her, running down her dress from her shoulders, over her breasts down to her entrance.

Almost with the appearance of coordinated thought, he suddenly pulled up the dress, exposing her shaved beauty clearly to Rob and Natalya, and she undid his trousers and took his length in her hands.

His meat was not as long as Rob's, but what it lacked in length it made up for in girth, and as Natalya looked back at it, she wondered what it would feel like to have such an implement pressed hard into her.

Rob could feel his own penis almost explode with arousal as he watched the strangers as she backed into the railings. The guy lifted her with his hands under her thighs and then lowered her down onto his pole. She screamed out with pleasure as he entered her and within seconds was panting with glee as he moved back and forth in and out of her.

Rob resumed his own movements, his feeling twice as sensitive as it slipped in and out of Natalya's sopping slit. Neither couple was able to focus entirely upon themselves, and all of them remained entranced by watching what the other couple was doing. Natalya was suddenly dissatisfied with her position looking away from the scene over the

Thames. She pulled herself away from Rob and felt his length disengage from her, and then bounce into her bum, wet against her skin.

She wanted to enjoy the absolute licentious nature of the moment and decided to see whether the other couple was as bold as they seemed. She turned to face Rob, letting him see her lightly trimmed pubes, now sodden with their essence. She then discarded her jacket, placing it carefully on the railings next to them. This left her standing on the darkened pier, her lace dress pulled up to expose everything below her navel, and her nipples formed into hard cones, poking at the lace.

She took Rob by the hand and then walked towards the other couple and smiled at them as they both watched her wearily, obviously wondering what she would do next.

If you enjoyed this sample then look for <u>She Made Him Do It</u>.

# KERRY JAMES
## HISTORICAL ROMANCE

# TIME ONCE MORE *for*
# MARILYN
## CAPTIVATED & REKINDLED

Nineteen-fifty-seven was not a particularly notable year for the world, or for the inhabitants of the United Kingdom. Of course, there were quite a few people who would look back and say. "That was a good year, a very good year." But for many it was just another year. There were births, quite a few into poverty and starvation and the law of averages dictated that an equal number died possibly from that same poverty and starvation. In October the Soviets would launch the first orbiting satellite and the word 'Sputnik' became part of every language. This was a shock for every developed nation, particularly the Americans, as no one thought that the Russians had the technology to achieve that feat. We all got a year older, although some, like my mother celebrated her birthday and resolutely remained thirty five, ignoring the fact that she was born in nineteen eleven. The Spartan existence, we had known in these isles during WW2 and immediately after had relaxed and our family along with many others was enjoying a more comfortable life.

Our Prime Minister had told us we were never having it so good. At that time, in our innocence we tended to believe the politicians; later the scales would drop from our eyes. For the moment we went along with this fantasy. Most families had a television now and a refrigerator and if those were the yardstick by which to judge then we were indeed better off. There were jobs for all those who wanted to work and State Benefits for those who declined that activity. The Unions flexed their muscles to introduce socialist principles into Industry. They battled for those whom they called 'the workers' implying by inference that anyone who wasn't unionized was a shirker or a parasite or both. The 'workers' ironically spent more time not working; as their shop stewards frequently called them out on strike for the flimsiest of reasons. The Unions espoused democracy yet rarely let their members vote on strike action. The conflict between the workers and the management was a running battle that went on and on, ensuring years later the almost complete demise of British industry. If we were having it so good, it was a Fool's Paradise. However, for the moment we basked in the sunshine.

It was a surprise, therefore when my dad announced that the family was going away for a week's holiday. The surprise was that I was included. When I was young, we had family holidays. A week or two in the West Country, travelling there by train with accommodation provided by the euphemistically described 'Guest House'. A Guest House was one very small step above a boarding house. The furnishings were better, but the rules were the same, whatever the weather you had to leave during the day and not return before five o'clock. You were provided with bed, breakfast, and an evening meal, no early morning or afternoon tea. For me, the journey by train was the highlight. We travelled by 'The Cornish Riviera Express', the crack train of the Great Western, which, in nineteen forty-eight became the Western Region of British Railways. In those days it was still hauled by a steam engine, either a 'King' or 'Castle', gleaming in Brunswick Green with brass trim and copper burnished all glittering in the light. It was supposed to run non-stop to Truro in Cornwall, but it did stop at Plymouth. Not in the station, but just outside so the engine could be changed. The 'Kings' and 'Castles' were too heavy for the Royal Albert Bridge over the Tamar so they were changed for another, lighter locomotive. It was only later that I understood that during the holiday season there were at least three or four trains that left Paddington in the space of an hour and a half, all called 'The Cornish Riviera Express'. That did mar a little the pride in travelling on that special train. In the mid-fifties, my dad took a new job; moving the whole family from the London area to the Midlands. His position also allowed him a company car for private as well as business use. So the romance of the Cornish Riviera was now history.

For three or four years prior to this, my parents had taken advantage of the burgeoning package holiday offers, and would go off to Spain or Italy with my younger sister. I was left at home with a cash bribe from my father to ensure that I would eat properly for the two weeks they were away. I didn't think they were rejecting me; it was probably because they didn't know what to do with an early teenager at the time. Now it would seem that at eighteen, I was acceptable company once more. Those last three years had transformed me from a gangling strip of a boy at five feet six, into a relatively decent looking man of five foot ten with dark brown hair and a face that could be described as reasonable rather than handsome.

The hotel was quite large with most of the amenities that you would expect. It was situated on a promontory called Daddyhole Plain and overlooked the sweep of the bay and the town. I assumed from the look of the place that it had once been the palatial home of some rich man and had been converted into a hotel with extensions for bedrooms and function rooms. The conversion had been done piecemeal so finding your way about was somewhat difficult as corridors seemingly leading in the right direction would take a sudden turn and take you to a place you didn't want to be. My parents and my sister had rooms on the first floor where the best rooms were. My sister got one of those so they could keep an eye on her she was only eleven at the time. I had a single room on the third floor. I got there by taking the main staircase up to the first floor, walking down the long corridor, then climbing another, less grand staircase to the second where I had to reverse the walk on the first floor to yet another, even smaller staircase that would take me to my floor. The room had a quaint ceiling, sloping within the confines of a gable. From the window I had an interesting view over the roofs and back gardens, but not a glimpse of anything remotely like a beach or sea. There was a wash basin with hot and cold running in the room, but for any other needs I would have to go down the corridor. The concept of en-suite facilities was unknown to the majority of hotels in the UK. That changed eventually with dire consequences for those hotels that didn't adapt. I didn't mind the disparity in accommodation; I got some privacy to indulge whatever my teenage hormones could discover for me. As it happened, I didn't have to go looking; adventure in the shape of the female variety came looking for me…

If you enjoyed this sample then look for **Time Once More For Marilyn**.

# JACK RYDER

# The Step Monster MILF

## TABOO EROTICA

I was still moaning and panting for air as Jane lifted her face away from my still oozing prick. She had her mouth closed, but she had a huge grin on her face as she sat up. Jane winked at me then opened her mouth to show me that her mouth was full of my thick white jism. A little bit of it drooled down her chin and dripped down onto her breasts. Then, she closed her mouth and made a gulping noise as she swallowed it all.

"Damn...that was nasty sexy," I groaned.

"That was yummy," Jane giggled. "Did you like it when I was nasty for you?" She asked it in a sort of naughty tone. She moved forward so my oozing dick was right between her tits. "Next time...maybe I'll fuck you with these tits that you love so much," she added. Jane was mashing her tits back and forth on my cock and the oozing fluid smeared all over her chest.

"That would be a lot better than just jerking off when you think about them, Huh?" she taunted me.

"Oh Yes, Jane...Oh God yes, God yes," I moaned. It thrilled me that Jane knew that I think about her when I jerk off. She moved forward and we kissed passionately for several moments. I was surprised that the saltiness of my jizz in her mouth did not bother me one bit.

I had started fondling and squeezing on Jane's cum slick tits while we were kissing. When she finally moved back after the kiss, I pulled her forward and began to suck on her tits greedily. "Oh Peter...Oooooh Peter," she purred. Jane's hands grabbed my head and she mashed my face harder into her chest. "Yes baby, Ooooh yes," she moaned. I felt her body shudder as I gently bit down on one of her nipples and then pulled on it so it stretched forward. "Ooooh Peter, Yesss, Yesss," she gasped.

I repeated this several more times over the next several moments on both of her nipples. "My pussy is so fucking wet," she moaned throatily. I was pleased to find that her panties were completely saturated with her juice when I slipped my hand between her legs and rubbed my palm against the crotch of her panties. "Oooooh Peeeeeeter," she moaned when I rubbed my fingers up and down her gash.

I pushed Jane's dress up to her waist then ripped her panties down to her feet. "I'm going to fuck you, Jane." I was surprised by the deep lust in my voice as I tossed her panties on the floor.

"Oh, Peeeeeter," she gasped again when I shoved my face against her cunt and started slurping at her dripping sex hole. "Yes Peter...Yes, Yes," she groaned. I could feel her body quivering as I greedily drilled my tongue in and out of her gash. "Oooh Yes, Oooh Yes, Oooh Yes," she wailed.

My dick was fully erect within a few minutes and I was sex drunk from the intoxicating scent of her muskiness. I scooted forward and shoved my 8 inch prick into her hole till I was completely buried in her pussy.

"Ooooooh, Peeeeeeter!" It was a deep husky primal sort of moan. I held myself buried inside of her for several moments to enjoy this first time of being inside my step mother's cunt.

The sloppy wetness of her pussy was exquisite as she trembled beneath me. I could feel Jane's pussy contracting around my prick and every pulsation of my dick inside of her. "Oooh, Jane," I gasped. I had to smile as I remembered saying that as I emptied my balls inside of Sara's tight virgin cunt.

"You feel so fucking good," Jane moaned softly. "Take me, Peter. Fuck me," she moaned in that deep husky voice again. I pulled my dick almost all the way out and slammed it back in forcefully. "Oh my God yes," she bellowed.

Squish, squish, squish, squish...Jane's pussy was so drenched that her juice squirted out all over each time I thrust into her. Because I had already came in Jane's mouth, I was able to fuck her savagely for nearly twenty minutes. By the time I was ready to climax, Jane was so winded from her long series of orgasms, that she suddenly went limp beneath me as she passed out for a couple of seconds.

I was just at the verge of my climax when Jane passed out. When she went limp, her bladder let loose and she wet herself just as my dick began to spasm inside of her. The sloppy sensation of her urine gushing out of her thrilled me so much that my cock absolutely exploded into Jane's quivering womb. My dick squirted four huge wads of cum deep into her womanhood. "Yes, baby, give it to me," Jane moaned softly as she felt my cum flooding into her.

"I'm never going to forget this night," I whispered as I leaned forward and kissed her cheek.

"That is so sweet that you will remember our first time," she whispered back.

"And it was my very first blow job and the first time I ever ate pussy," I informed her softly.

"Oh Peter, I will remember that too, baby." Then she pulled me down and kissed me very passionately.

When we got up off the couch, there was a huge urine stain in the middle of the sofa cushion and globs of cum that oozed out of her gash. Jane pulled her dress off over her head and tossed it on top of the mess. "I'll clean that up tomorrow before your dad gets home," she giggled. I felt elated when she held my hand and led me to her bedroom completely naked. But I also felt sad that my asshole father would be returning just as this was beginning with Jane.

"I'm sorry that I hated you," I whispered in her ear when we were in the bed.

"Don't be silly," Jane chuckled. "You never hated me at all." I could see a genuine love in her eyes as she peered into mine. "You were just trying to block what you really wanted from me." Her fingers were now brushing up and down my chest. "What happened tonight is what you really wanted all along." She leaned forward and kissed my cheek. "I was just waiting for you to figure it out," she added.

"How did you know all of this?" I asked her softly.

Jane just laughed cheerfully. "Because I've heard you jerking off in your room almost every day after you stare at my tits," she giggled. "I heard you moan my name and I found my panties that you used to jerk off on." My face was now turning red. "And I saw you masturbating when you watched me in the shower too," she informed me.

My face was now beet red as she continued to gaze into my eyes. "But that's okay, baby," she chuckled. "I left those panties for you to find and I left the door open so you could see me naked in the shower," she told me softly. "Truth is...I masturbated for you too, baby," she whispered. "My pussy got so wet when you looked at my tits that I would go finger myself as soon as you left the house every morning," she confessed. "So, I decided to try something...to attract your attention." She kissed my cheek. "This was better than I ever dreamed," she whispered.

It felt wonderful as we laid there and cuddled. Jane gently stroked my back as I kissed her neck and chest tenderly. "I think...I could fall in love with you, Jane..."

If you enjoyed this sample then look for **The Step Monster MILF**.

www.ingramcontent.com/pod-product-compliance
Lightning Source LLC
Chambersburg PA
CBHW071415170626
46811CB00003B/1412